A Collection of Short Stories from the

Bystander & Morning Post

Including 'A Shot in the Dark', 'The Holy War', 'The Pond', and Many More

By

Hector Hugh Munro

(Saki)

British Library Cataloguing-in-Publication Data
A catalogue record for this book is available from the
British Library

Hector Hugh Munro

Hector Hugh Munro was born in Akyab, Burma in 1870. He was raised by aunts in North Devon, England, before returning to Burma in his early twenties to join the Colonial Burmese Military Police. Later, Munro returned once more to England, where he embarked on his career as a journalist, becoming well-known for his satirical 'Alice in Westminster' political sketches, which appeared in the *Westminster Gazette.* Munro's first longer work, a historical treatise entitled *The Rise of the Russian Empire* appeared in 1900. His first collection of short stories, *Not-so-Stories,* was published two years later. After a stint as a foreign correspondent in the Balkans and Russia, Munro published *The Chronicles of Clovis* (1911), another collection of short stories which featured his most famous hero, Clovis. During World War I, he reached the rank of Lance Sergeant, and penned a number of short stories from the trenches. However, he was killed by a German sniper in November of 1916, aged 45. Arguably better-remembered by his pen name, 'Saki', Munro is now considered a master of the short story, with tales such as 'The Open Window' regarded as examples of the form at its finest.

Contents

Clovis On The Alleged Romance Of Business

"It is the fashion nowadays," said Clovis, "to talk about the romance of Business. There isn't such a thing. The romance has all been the other way, with the idle apprentice, the truant, the run-away, the individual who couldn't be bothered with figures and book-keeping and left business to look after itself. I admit that a grocer's shop is one of the most romantic and thrilling things I have ever happened upon, but the romance and thrill are centred in the groceries, not the grocer. The citron and spices and nuts and dates, the barrelled anchovies and Dutch cheeses, the jars of caviar and chest of tea, they carry the mind away to Levantine coast towns and tropic shores, to the Old World wharfs and quays of the Low Countries, to dusty Astrachan and far Cathay; if the grocer's apprentice has any romance in him it is not a business education he gets behind the grocer's counter, it is a standing invitation to dream and to wander, and to remain poor. As a child such places as South America and Asia Minor were brought painstakingly under my notice, the names of their principal rivers and the heights of their chief mountain peaks were committed to my memory. and I was earnestly enjoined to consider them as parts of the world that I lived in; it was only when I visited a large well-stocked grocer's shop that I realized that they certainly existed. Such galleries of romance and fascination are not bequeathed to us by the business man; he is only the dull custodian, who talks glibly of Spanish olives and Rangoon rice, a Spain that he has never known or wished to know, a Rangoon that he has never imagined or could imagine. It was the unledgered wanderer, the careless-hearted seafarer, the aimless outcast, who opened up new trade routes, tapped new markets, brought home samples or cargoes of new edibles and unknown condiments. It was they who brought the glamour and romance to the threshold of business life, where it was promptly reduced to pounds, shillings and pence; invoiced, double-entried, quoted, written off, and so forth; most of these terms are probably wrong, but a little inaccuracy sometimes serves tons of explanation.

"On the other side of the account there is the industrious apprentice, who grew up into the business man, married early and worked late, and lived, thousands and thousands of him, in little villas outside big towns. He is buried by the thousand in Kensal Green and other large cemeteries; any romance that was ever in him was buried prematurely in shop and warehouse and office. Whenever I feel in the least tempted to be business-like or methodical or even decently industrious I go to Kensal Green and look at the graves of those who died in business."

THE POND

Mona had always regarded herself as cast for the tragic life; her name, her large dark eyes, and the style of hairdressing that best suited her, all contributed to support that outlook on life. She habitually wore the air of one who has seen trouble, or, at any rate, expects to do so very shortly; and she was accustomed to speak of the Angel of Death almost as other people would speak of their chauffeur waiting around the corner to fetch them at the appointed moment. Fortune-tellers, noting this tendency in her disposition, invariably hinted at something in her fate which they would not care to speak about too explicitly. "You will marry the man of your choice, but afterwards you will pass through strange fires," a Bond Street two-guinea palm-oilist had told her. "Thank you," said Mona, "for your plain speaking. But I have known it always."

In marrying John Waddacombe. Mona had mated herself with a man who shared none of her intimacy with the shadowy tragedies of what she called the half-seen world. He had the substantial tragedies of his own world to bother about, without straining his eyes for the elusive and dubious distractions belonging to a sphere that lay entirely beyond his range of vision; or, for the matter of that, his range of interests. Potato blight, swine fever, the Government's land legislation, and other pests of the farm absorbed his attention as well as his energies, and even if he had admitted the possibility of such a disease as soul-sickness, of which Mona recognised eleven distinct varieties, most of them incurable, he would probably have prescribed a fortnight at the seaside as the most hopeful and natural remedy. There was no disguising the fact, John Waddacombe was of the loam, loamy. If he had cared to go into politics he would have been known inevitably as honest John Waddacombe, and after that there is nothing more to be said.

Two days, or thereabouts, after her marriage, Mona had made the tragic discovery that she was yoked to a life-partner with whom she had little in common, and from whom she could expect nothing in the way of sympathetic understanding. Anyone else, knowing both her and John and their respective temperaments, could her have advanced her that information the moment that the engagement was announced. John was fond of her in his own way, and she, in her quite different way, was more than a little fond of him; but they trafficked in ideas that had scarcely a common language.

Mona set out on her married life with the expectation of being misunderstood, and after a while John arrived at the rather obvious conclusion that he didn't understand her — and was content to "leave it at that". His wife was at first irritated and then disheartened by his attitude of stolid indifference. "Least said, soonest mended," was his comfortable doctrine, which failed woefully when applied to Mona's share of the reticence. She was unhappy and perturbed about their lack of soul-fellowship; why couldn't he be decently distressed about it also? From being at first theatrically miserable she became more seriously affected. The morbid strain in her character found at last something tangible to feed on, and brought a good appetite to the feeding. While John was busy and moderately happy with his farm troubles, Mona was dull, unoccupied, and immoderately unhappy with her own trouble.

It was at this time, in the course of one of her moody, listless rambles, that she came across the pond. In the high chalky soil of the neighbourhood, standing water was a rarity; with the exception of the artificially made duck-pond at the farm and one or two cattle pools, Mona knew of no other for miles around. It stood in a clay "pocket" in the heart of a neglected beech plantation on the steep side of a hill, a dark, evil-looking patch of water, fenced round and overspread with gloomy yews and monstrous decaying beeches. It was not a cheerful spot, and such picturesqueness as it possessed was all on the side of melancholy; the only human suggestion that could arise in connection with the pool was the idea of a dead body floating on its surface. Mona took to the place with an instantaneous sense of fascination; it suited her temperament, and it mightily suited her mood. Nearly all her walks led her to the beech wood, and the Mecca of the wood was always the still, dark pond, with its suggestion of illimitable depths, its silence, its air of an almost malignant despondency. If one could indulge in such a flight of fancy as to imagine a hill rejoicing, or a valley smiling, one could certainly picture the pond wearing a sullen, evil scowl.

Mona wove all sorts of histories about the pool, and in most of them there was some unhappy, fate-buffeted soul who hung wearily over its beckoning depths and finally floated in sombre spectacular repose among the weeds on its surface, and each time that she reshaped the story she identified the victim more and more with herself. She would stand or sit on the steeply inclined bank that overhung the pond on every side, peering down into the water and reflecting on the consequences that would follow a slip of her foot or an incautious venturing over-near the edge. How long would she struggle in those unfathomed weed-grown depths before she lay as picturesquely still as the drowned heroine of her tale-weavings, and how long would she float there in peace, with the daylight and moonlight reaching down to her through the over-arching catafalque of yew and beech, before searchers discovered her resting-place, and haled her body away to the sordid necessities of inquest and burial? The idea of ending her despondencies and soul troubles in that dark, repose-inviting pool took firmer and clearer shape; there seemed a spirit lurking in its depths and smiling on its surface that beckoned her to lean further and yet further over its edge, to stand more and more rashly on the steep slope that overhung it. She took a subtle pleasure in marking how the fascination grew on her with each visit; how the dread of the catastrophe that she was courting grew less and less. Every time that she reluctantly tore herself away from the spot there seemed a half-jeering, half-reproachful murmur in the air around her, "Why not to-day?"

And then, at a timely moment, John Waddacombe, hearty as an ox, and seemingly proof against weather exposure, fell suddenly and critically ill with a lung attack that nearly triumphed over doctors and nurses and his own powers of stubborn resistance. Mona did her fair share of the nursing while the case was critical, fighting with greater zeal against the death that threatened her husband than she had shown in combatting the suggestion of self-destruction that had gained so insidious a hold on her. And when the convalescent stage had been reached she found John, weak and rather fretful as he was after his long experience of the sick-room, far more lovable and sympathetic than he had been in the days of his vigour. The barriers of reserve and mutual impatience had been broken down, and husband and wife found that they had more in common than they had once thought possible. Mona forgot the pond, or thought of it only with a shudder; a healthy contempt for her morbid weakness and silliness had begun to assert itself. John was not the only one of them who was going through a period of convalescence.

The self-pity and the coquetry with self-destruction had passed away under the stress of new sympathies and interests; the morbid undercurrent was part of Mona's nature, and was not to cast out at a moment's notice. It was the prompting of this undercurrent that led her, one day in the autumn, to pay a visit to the spot where she had toyed so weakly with stupid, evil ideas and temptations. It would be, she felt, a curious sensation to renew acquaintance with the place now that its fascination and potential tragedy had been destroyed. In outward setting it was more desolate and gloom-shrouded than ever; the trees had lost their early autumnal magnificence, and rain had soaked the fallen beech-leaves into a paste of dark slush under foot. Amid the nakedness of their neighbours, the yews stood out thick, and black, and forbidding, and the sickly growth of fungoid things showed itself prominently amid the rotting vegetation. Mona peered down at the dark, ugly pool, and shuddered to think that she could ever have contemplated an end so horrible as choking and gasping to death in those foul, stagnant depths, with their floating surface of slime and creeping water insects and rank weed-growth. And then the thing that she recoiled from in disgust seemed to rise up towards her as though to drag her down in a long-deferred embrace. Her feet had slipped on the slithery surface of sodden leaves and greasy clay, and she was sliding helplessly down the steep bank to where it dropped sheer into the pool. She clutched and clawed frantically at yielding roots and wet, slippery earth, and felt the weight of her body pull her downward with ever-increasing momentum. The hideous pool, whose fascination she had courted and slighted, was gaping in readiness for her; even if she had been a swimmer there would have been little chance for her in those weed-tangled depths, and John would find her there, as once she had almost wished — John who had loved her and learned to love her better than ever; John whom she loved with all her heart. She raised her voice to call his name again and again, but she knew he was a mile or two away, busy with the farm life that once more claimed his devoted attention. She felt the bank slide away from her in a dark, ugly smear, and heard the small stones and twigs that she had dislodged fall with soft splashes into the water at her feet; above her, far above her it seemed, the yews spread their sombre branches like the roof-span of a crypt.

* * * * *

"Heavens alive, Mona, where did you get all that mud?" asked John in some pardonable astonishment. "Have you been playing catch-as-catch-can with the pigs? You're splashed up to the eyes in it."

"I slipped into a pond," said Mona.

"What, into the horse-pond?" asked John.

"No, a pond out in one of the woods," she explained.

"I didn't know there was such a thing for miles around," said John.

"Well, perhaps it would be an exaggeration to call it a pond," said Mona with a faint trace of resentment in her voice; "it's only about an inch and a half deep."

The Bystander, 21st February, 1912

A SHOT IN THE DARK

Philip Sletherby settled himself down in an almost empty railway carriage, with the pleasant consciousness of being embarked on an agreeable and profitable pilgrimage. He was bound for Brill Manor, the country residence of his newly achieved acquaintance, Mrs. Saltpen-Jago. Honoria Saltpen-Jago was a person of some social importance in London, of considerable importance and influence in the county of Chalkshire. The county of Chalkshire, or, at any rate, the eastern division of it, was of immediate personal interest to Philip Sletherby; it was held for the Government in the present Parliament by a gentleman who did not intend to seek re-election, and Sletherby was under serious consideration by the party managers as his possible successor. The majority was not a large one, and the seat could not be considered safe for a Ministerial candidate, but there was an efficient local organisation, and with luck the seat might be held. The Saltpen-Jago influence was not an item which could be left out of consideration, and the political aspirant had been delighted at meeting Honoria at a small and friendly luncheon-party, still more gratified when she had asked him down to her country house for the following Friday-to-Tuesday. He was obviously "on approval", and if he could secure the goodwill of his hostess he might count on the nomination as an assured thing. If he failed to find favour in her eyes — well, the local leaders would probably cool off in their embryo enthusiasm for him.

Among the passengers dotted about on the platform, awaiting their respective trains, Sletherby espied a club acquaintance, and beckoned him up to the carriage-window for a chat.

"Oh, you're staying with Mrs. Saltpen-Jago for the week-end, are you? I expect you'll have a good time; she has the reputation of being an excellent hostess. She'll be useful to you, too, if that Parliamentary project — hullo, you're off. Good-bye."

Sletherby waved good-bye to his friend, pulled up the window, and turned his attention to the magazine lying on his lap. He had scarcely glanced at a couple of pages, however, when a smothered curse caused him to glance hastily at the only other occupant of the carriage. His travelling companion was a young man of about two-and-twenty, with dark hair, fresh complexion, and the blend of smartness and disarray that marks the costume of a "nut" who is bound on a rustic holiday. He was engaged in searching furiously and ineffectually for some elusive or non-existent object; from time to time he dug a sixpenny bit out of a waistcoat pocket and stared at it ruefully, then recommenced the futile searching operations. A cigarette-case, matchbox, latchkey, silver pencil case, and railway ticket were turned out on to the seat beside him, but none of these articles seemed to afford him satisfaction; he cursed again, rather louder than before.

The vigorous pantomime did not draw forth any remark from Sletherby, who resumed his scrutiny of the magazine.

"I say!" exclaimed a young voice presently, "didn't I hear you say you were going down to stay with Mrs. Saltpen-Jago at Brill Manor? What a coincidence! My mater, you know. I'm coming on there on Monday evening, so we shall meet. I'm quite a stranger; haven't seen the mater for six months at least. I was away yachting last time she was in Town. I'm Bertie, the second son, you know. I say, it's an awfully lucky coincidence that I should run across someone who knows the mater just at this particular moment. I've done an damned awkward thing."

"You've lost something, haven't you?" said Sletherby

"Not exactly, but left behind, which is almost as bad; just as inconvenient, anyway. I've come away without my sovereign-purse, with four quid in it, all my worldly wealth for the moment. It was in my pocket all right, just before I was starting, and then I wanted to seal a letter, and the sovereign-purse happens to have my crest on it, so I whipped it out to stamp the seal with, and, like a double-distilled idiot, I must have left it on the table. I had some silver loose in my pocket, but after I'd paid for a taxi and my ticket I'd only got this forlorn little sixpence left. I'm stopping at a little country inn near Brondquay for three days' fishing; not a soul knows me there, and my week-end bill, and tips, and cab to and from the station, and my ticket on to Brill, that will mount up to two or three quid, won't it? If you wouldn't mind lending me two pound ten, or three for preference, I shall be awfully obliged. It will pull me out of no end of a hole."

"I think I can manage that," said Sletherby, after a moment's hesitation.

"Thanks awfully. It's jolly good of you. What a lucky thing for me that I should have chanced across one of the mater's friends. It will be a lesson to me not to leave my exchequer lying about anywhere, when it ought to be in my pocket. I suppose the moral of the whole thing is don't try and convert things to purposes for which they weren't intended. Still, when a sovereign-purse has your crest on it—"

"What is your crest, by the way?" Sletherby asked, carelessly.

"Not a very common one," said the youth; "a demi-lion holding a cross-crosslet in its paw."

"When your mother wrote to me, giving me a list of trains, she had, if I remember rightly, a greyhound courant on her notepaper," observed Sletherby. There was a tinge of coldness in his voice.

"That is the Jago crest," responded the youth promptly; "the demi-lion is the Saltpen crest. We have the right to use both, but I always use the demi-lion, because, after all, we are really Saltpens."

There was silence for a moment or two, and the young man began to collect his fishing tackle and other belongings from the rack.

"My station is the next one," he announced.

"I've never met your mother," said Sletherby suddenly, "though we've corresponded several times. My introduction to her was through political friends. Does she resemble you at all in feature? I should rather like to be able to pick her out if she happened to be on the platform to meet me."

"She's supposed to be like me. She has the same dark brown hair and high colour; it runs in her family. I say, this is where I get out."

"Good-bye," said Sletherby.

"You've forgotten the three quid," said the young man, opening the carriage-door and pitching his suit-case on to the platform.

"I've no intention of lending you three pounds, or three shillings," said Sletherby severely.

"But you said–"

"I know I did. My suspicions hadn't been roused then, though I hadn't necessarily swallowed your story. The discrepancy about the crests put me on my guard, notwithstanding the really brilliant way in which you accounted for it. Then I laid a trap for you; I told you that I had never met Mrs. Saltpen-Jago. As a matter of fact I met her at lunch on Monday last. She is a pronounced blonde."

The train moved on, leaving the soi-disant cadet of the Saltpen-Jago family cursing furiously on the platform.

"Well, he hasn't opened his fishing expedition by catching a flat," chuckled Sletherby. He would have an entertaining story to recount at dinner that evening, and his clever little trap would earn him applause as a man of resource and astuteness. He was still telling his adventure in imagination to an attentive audience of dinner guests when the train drew up at his destination. On the platform he was greeted sedately by a tall footman, and noisily by Claude People, K.C., who had apparently travelled down by the same train.

"Hullo, Sletherby! You spending the week-end at Brill? Good. Excellent. We'll have a round of golf together to-morrow; I'll give you your revenge for Hoylake. Not a bad course here, as inland courses go. Ah, here we are; here's the car waiting for us, and very nice, too!"

The car which won the K.C.'s approval was a sumptuous-looking vehicle, which seemed to embody the last word in elegance, comfort, and locomotive power. Its graceful lines and symmetrical design masked the fact that it was an enormous wheeled structure, combining the features of a hotel lounge and an engine-room.

"Different sort of vehicle to the post-chaise in which our grandfathers used to travel, eh?" exclaimed the lawyer appreciatively. And for Sletherby's benefit he began running over the chief points of perfection in the fitting and mechanism of the car.

Sletherby heard not a single word, noted not one of the details that were being expounded to him. His eyes were fixed on the door panel, on which were displayed two crests: a greyhound courant and a demi-lion holding in its paw a cross-crosslet.

The K.C. was not the sort of man to notice an absorbed silence on the part of a companion. He had been silent himself for nearly an hour in the train, and his tongue was making up for lost time. Political gossip, personal anecdote, and general observation flowed from him in an uninterrupted stream as the car sped along the country roads; from the inner history of the Dublin labour troubles and the private life of the Prince Designate of Albania he progressed with an easy volubility to an account of an alleged happening at the ninth hole at Sandwich, and a verbatim report of a remark made by the Duchess of Pathshire at a Tango tea. Just as the car turned in at the Brill entrance gates the K.C. captured Sletherby's attention by switching his remarks to the personality of their hostess.

"Brilliant woman, level-headed, a clear thinker, knows exactly when to take up an individual or a cause, exactly when to let him or it drop. Influential woman, but spoils herself and her chances by being too restless. No repose. Good appearance, too, till she made that idiotic change."

"Change?" queried Sletherby, "what change?"

"What change? You don't mean to say– Oh, of course, you've only known her just lately. She used to have beautiful dark brown hair, which went very well with her fresh complexion; then one day, about five weeks ago, she electrified everybody by appearing as a brilliant blonde. Quite ruined her looks. Here we are. I say, what's the matter with you? You look rather ill."

The Bystander, 3rd December, 1913

A SACRIFICE TO NECESSITY

Alicia Pevenly sat on a garden seat in the rose-walk at Chopehanger, enjoying the valedictory mildness of a warm October morning, and experiencing the atmosphere of mental complacency that descends on a woman who has breakfasted well, is picturesquely dressed, and has reached forty-two in pleasant insidious stages. The loss of her husband some ten years ago had woven a thread of tender regret into her life-pattern, but for the most part she looked on the world and its ways with placid acquiescent amiability. The income on which she and her seventeen-year-old daughter lived and kept up appearances was small, almost inconveniently small, perhaps, but with due management and a little forethought it sufficed. Contriving and planning gained a certain amount of zest from the fact that there was only such a slender margin of shillings to be manipulated.

"There is all the difference in the world," Mrs. Pevenly would say to herself, "between being badly off and merely having to be careful."

Regarding her own personal affairs with a measured tranquillity, she did not let the larger events of the world disturb her peace of mind. She took a warm, but quite impersonal interest, in the marriage of Prince Arthur of Connaught, thereby establishing her claim to be considered a woman with broad sympathies and intelligently in touch with the age in which she lived. On the other hand, she was not greatly stirred by the question whether Ireland should or should not be given Home Rule, and she was absolutely indifferent as to where the southern frontier of Albania should be drawn or whether it should be drawn at all; if there had ever been a combative strain in her nature it had never been developed.

Mrs. Pevenly had finished her breakfast at about half-past nine, by which time her daughter had not put in an appearance; as the hostess and most of the members of the house-party were equally late, Beryl's slackness could not be regarded as a social sin, but her mother thought it was a pity to lose so much of the fine October morning. Beryl Pevenly had been described by someone as the "Flapper incarnate", and the label summed her up accurately. Her mother already recognised that she was disposed to be a law unto herself; what she did not yet realise was that Beryl was extremely likely to be a law-giver to any weaker character with whom she might come into contact.

"She is only a child yet," Mrs. Pevenly would say to herself, forgetting that seventeen and seventy are about the two most despotic ages of human life.

"Ah, finished breakfast at last!" she called out in mock reproof as her daughter came out to join her in the rose-walk; "if you had gone to bed in good time these last two evenings, as I did, you would not be so tired in the mornings. It has been so fresh and charming out here, while all you silly people have been lying in bed. I hope you weren't playing bridge for high stakes, my dear!"

There was a tired defiant look in Beryl's eyes that drew forth the anxious remark.

"Bridge? No, we started with a rubber or two the night before last," said Beryl, "but we switched off to baccarat. Rather a mistake for some of us."

"Beryl, you haven't been losing?" asked Mrs. Pevenly with increased anxiety in her voice.

"I lost quite a lot the first evening," said Beryl, "and as I couldn't possibly pay back my losses I simply punted the next evening to try and get them back; I've come to the conclusion that baccarat is not my game. I came a bigger cropper on the second evening than on the first."

"Beryl, this is awful! I've very angry with you. Tell me quickly, how much have you lost?"

Beryl looked at a slip of paper that she was twisting and untwisting in her hands.

"Three hundred and ten the first night, seven hundred and sixteen the second," she announced.

"Three hundred what?"

"Pounds."

"Pounds?", screamed the mother; "Beryl, I don't believe you. Why, that is a thousand pounds!"

"A thousand and twenty-six, to be exact," said Beryl.

Mrs. Pevenly was too frightened to cry.

"Where do you suppose," she asked, "that we could raise a thousand pounds, or anything like a thousand pounds? We are living at the top of our income, we are practising all sorts of economies, we simply couldn't subtract a thousand pounds from our little capital. It would ruin us."

"We should be socially ruined if it got about that we played for stakes that we couldn't or wouldn't pay; no one would ask us anywhere."

"How came you to do such a dreadful thing?" wailed the mother.

"Oh, it's no use asking those sort of questions," said Beryl; "the thing is done. I suppose I inherit a gambling instinct from some of you."

"You certainly don't," exclaimed Mrs. Pevenly hotly; "your father never touched cards or cared anything about horse-racing, and I don't know one game of cards from another."

"These things skip a generation sometimes, and come out all the stronger in the next batch," said Beryl; "how about that uncle of yours who used to get up a sweepstake every Sunday at school as to which of the Books of the Bible the text of the sermon would be taken from? If he wasn't a keen gambler I've never heard of one."

"Don't let's argue," faltered the elder woman, "let's think of what is to be done. How many people do you owe the money to?"

"Luckily it's all due to one person, Ashcombe Gwent," said Beryl; "he was doing nearly all the winning on both nights. He's rather a good sort in his way, but unluckily he isn't a bit well off, and one couldn't expect him to overlook the fact that money was owing to him. I fancy he's just as much of an adventurer as we are."

"We are not adventurers," protested Mrs. Pevenly.

"People who come to stay at country houses and play for stakes that they've no prospect of paying if they lose, are adventurers," said Beryl, who seemed determined to include her mother in any moral censure that might be applied to her own conduct.

"Have you said anything to him about the difficulty you are in?"

"I have. That's what I've come to tell you about. We had a talk this morning in the billiard-room after breakfast. It seems there is just one way out of the tangle. He's inclined to be amorous."

"Amorous!" exclaimed the mother.

"Matrimonially amorous," said the daughter; "in fact, without either of us having guessed it, it appears that he's the victim of an infatuation."

"He has certainly been polite and attentive," said Mrs. Pevenly; "he is not a man who says much, but he listens to what one has to say. And do you mean he really wants to marry–?"

"That is exactly what he does want," said Beryl. "I don't know that he is the sort of husband that one would rave about, but I gather that he has enough to live on — as much as we're accustomed to, anyhow, and he's quite presentable to look at. The alternative is selling out a big chunk of our little capital; I should have to go and be a governess or typewriter or something, and you would have to do needlework. From just making things do, and paying rounds of visits and having a fairly good time, we should sink suddenly to the position of distressed gentlefolk. I don't know what you think, but I'm inclined to consider that the marriage proposition is the least objectionable."

Mrs. Pevenly took out her handkerchief.

"How old is he?" she asked.

"Oh, thirty-seven or thirty-eight; a year or two older perhaps."

"Do you like him?"

Beryl laughed.

"He's not in the least my style," she said.

Mrs. Pevenly began to weep.

"What a deplorable situation," she sobbed; "what a sacrifice for the sake of a miserable sum of money and social considerations! To think that such a tragedy should happen in our family. I've often read about such things in books, a girl being forced to marry a man she didn't care about because of some financial disaster–"

"You shouldn't read such trashy books," pronounced Beryl.

"But now it's really happening!" exclaimed the mother; "my own child's life to be sacrificed by marriage to a man years older than herself, whom she doesn't care the least bit about, and because–"

"Look here," interrupted Beryl. "I don't seem to have made this clear. It isn't me that he wants to marry. 'Flappers' don't appeal to him, he told me. Mature womanhood is his particular line, and it's you that he's infatuated about."

"Me!"

For the second time that morning Mrs. Pevenly's voice rose to a scream.

"Yes, he said you were his ideal, a ripe, sun-warmed peach, delicious and desirable, and a lot of other metaphors that he probably borrowed from Swinburne or Edmund Jones. I told him that under other circumstances I shouldn't have held out much hope of his getting a favourable response from you, but that as we owed him a thousand and twenty-six pounds you would probably consider a matrimonial alliance the most convenient way of discharging the obligation. He's coming out to speak to you himself in a few minutes, but I thought I'd better come and prepare you first."

"But, my dear—"

"Of course, you hardly know the man, but I don't think that matters. You see, you've been married before and a second husband is always something of an anti-climax. Here is Ashcombe. I think I'd better leave you two together. You must have a lot you want to say to each other."

The wedding took place quietly some eight weeks later. The presents were costly, if not numerous, and consisted chiefly of a cancelled I.O.U., the gift of the bridegroom to the bride's daughter.

The Bystander, 15th October, 1913

A HOUSEING PROBLEM

"I'm in a frightful position," exclaimed Mrs. Duff-Chubleigh, sinking into an armchair and closing her eyes as though to shut out some distressing vision.

"Really? What has happened?" asked Mrs. Pallitson, preparing herself to hear some kitchen tragedy.

"The more one tries to make one's house-parties a success, the more one seems to court failure," was the tragical reply.

"I'm sure it's been most enjoyable so far," said the guest politely; "weather, of course, one can't count on, but otherwise I can't see anything has gone wrong. I was thinking you were to be congratulated."

Mrs. Duff-Chubleigh laughed harshly and bitterly.

"It was so nice having the Marchioness here," she said; "she's dull and she dresses badly, but people in these parts think no end of her, and, of course, it's rather a social score to get hold of her. It counts for a good deal to be in her good graces. And now she talks of leaving us at a moment's notice."

"Really? That is unfortunate, but I'm sure she'll be sure to leave such a charming–"

"She's not leaving in sorrow," said the hostess; "no — in anger."

"Anger?"

"Bobby Chermbacon called her, to her face, a moth-eaten old hen. That's not the sort of thing one says to a Marchioness, and I told him so afterwards. He said she was only a Marchioness by marriage, which is absurd, because, of course, no one is born an Marchioness. Anyway, he didn't apologise, and she says she won't stay under the same roof with him."

"Under the circumstances," said Mrs. Pallitson, promptly, "I think you might help Mr. Chermbacon to choose a nice early train back to Town. There's one that goes before lunch, and I expect his valet could get the packing act done in something under twenty minutes."

Mrs. Duff-Chubleigh rose in silence, went to the door, and carefully closed it. Then she spoke slowly and impressively, with the air of a Minister who is asking an economically minded Parliament for an increased Navy Vote.

"Bobbie Chermbacon is rich, quite rich, and one day he will be very much richer. His aunt can buy motor-cars as we might buy theatre-tickets, and he will be her chief heir. I am getting on in years, though I may not look it."

"You don't," Mrs. Pallitson assured her.

"Thank you; still, the fact remains. I'm getting on in years, and though I've a reasonable number of children of my own I've reached that time of life when a woman begins to feel a great longing for a son-in-law. Bobbie told Margaret last night that she had the eyes of a dreaming Madonna."

"Extravagance in language seems to be his besetting characteristic," said Mrs. Pallitson; "of course," she continued hastily, "I don't mean to say that Margaret hasn't the eyes of a dreaming Madonna. I think the simile excellent."

"There are many different kinds of Madonna," said Mrs. Duff-Chubleigh.

"Exactly, but it's rather outspoken language for such short acquaintance. As I say, he seems to be a rather outspoken young man."

"Ah, but he said more than that; he said she reminded him of Gaby What's-her-name, you know, the fascinating actress that the King of Spain admires so much."

"Portugal," murmured Mrs. Pallitson.

"And he didn't confine himself to saying pretty things," continued the mother eagerly; "actions speak stronger than words. He gave her some exquisite orchids to wear at dinner last night. They were from our orchid-house, but, still, he went to the trouble of picking them."

"That shows a certain amount of devotion," agreed Mrs. Pallitson.

"And he said he adored chestnut hair," continued Mrs. Duff-Chubleigh; "Margaret's hair is a very beautiful shade of chestnut."

"He's known her for a very short time," said Mrs. Pallitson.

"It's always been chestnut," exclaimed Mrs. Duff-Chubleigh.

"Oh, I didn't mean that; I meant that the conquest was sudden, not the colour of the hair. These sudden infatuations are often the most genuine, I believe. A man sees someone for the first time, and knows at once that it is the one person he's been looking for."

"Well, you see the frightful position I'm in. Either the Marchioness leaves in a fury, or I've got to turn Bobbie adrift just as he and Margaret are getting on so very well. It will nip the whole thing in the bud. I didn't sleep a wink last night. I ate nothing for breakfast. If I'm found floating in the carp-pond, you, at least, will know the reason why."

"It's certainly a dreadful situation," said Mrs. Pallitson; "how would it be," she added slowly and reflectively, "if I were to ask Margaret and Bobbie over to our place for the remainder of the Marchioness's stay? My husband has got a men's party, but we could easily expand it. Out of all your guests you could subtract three without unduly diminishing your number. We could pretend that it was an old arrangement."

"Do you mind if I kiss you?" asked Mrs. Duff-Chubleigh; "after this we must call each other by our Christian names. Mine is Elizabeth."

"There I must object," said Mrs. Pallitson, who had submitted to the kiss; "there is dignity and charm in the name Elizabeth, but my godparents christened me Celeste. When a woman weighs as much as I do—"

"I'm sure you don't," exclaimed her hostess, in defiant disregard of logic.

"And inherits a very uncertain temper," resumed Mrs. Pallitson, "there is a distinct flavour of incongruity in answering to the name Celeste."

"You are doing a heavenly thing, and I think the name most appropriate; I shall always call you by it."

"I'm afraid we haven't an orchid-house," said Mrs. Pallitson, "but there are some rather choice tuberoses in the hothouse."

"Margaret's favourite flower!" exclaimed Mrs. Duff-Chubleigh.

Mrs. Pallitson repressed a sigh. She was fond of tuberoses herself.

The day after the transplanting of Bobbie and Margaret, Mrs. Duff-Chubleigh was called to the telephone.

"Is that you, Elizabeth?" came the voice of Mrs. Pallitson; "you must have Bobbie back. Don't say it's impossible, you must. The Bishop of Sokotra, my husband's uncle, is staying here. Sokotra, never mind how it's spelt. Bobbie told him last night what he thought of Christian missions; I've often said the same thing myself, but never to a Bishop. Nor have I expressed it in quite such offensive language. The Bishop refuses to stay another night under the same roof as Bobbie. He, the Bishop, is not merely an uncle, but a bachelor uncle, with private means. It's all very well to say he show a tolerant and charitable spirit; charity begins at home, and this is a Colonial Bishop. Sokotra, I keep telling you; it doesn't matter where it is, the point is that the Bishop is here, and we can't allow him to leave us in a temper."

"How about the Marchioness?" shrilled Mrs. Duff-Chubleigh at her end of the 'phone, having first carefully glanced around to see that nobody was within hearing distance of her remarks. "She's just as important to me as the Bishop of Scooter, or wherever it is, is to you. I don't know why he should take such absurd unreasonable offence because Christian missions were unfavourably criticised; anyone might express an opinion on a subject of that sort, even to a Colonial Bishop. It's a very different thing being called to your face a moth-eaten old hen. I hear she is going to give a hunt ball at Cloudly this winter, and it's quite probable that she'll ask me over there for it. And now you want me to ruin everything and have a most unpleasant contretemps by taking that boy back under my roof. You can't expect it of me. Besides, we can't keep shifting Mr. Chermbacon backwards and forwards as though he was the regulator of an erratic clock. What do you say?"

"The Bishop won't stay another night unless Bobbie goes to-night," came over the phone in hard relentless tones. "I've told Bobbie he must leave first thing after lunch, and I've ordered the motor to be ready for him. Margaret can follow to-morrow."

Then there followed a pitiless silence at the Pallitson end of the telephone. Vainly Mrs. Duff-Chubleigh rang up again and again, and put the fruitless and despairing question "Are you there?" to the cold emptiness of unresponsive space. The Pallitsons had cut themselves off.

"The telephone is the coward's weapon," muttered Mrs. Duff-Chubleigh furiously; "these heavy blonde women are always a mass of selfishness."

Then she sat down to write a telegram, as a last appeal to Celeste's better feelings.

Am having carp taken out of fish-pond. I can face drowning, but will not be nibbled.–ELIZABETH."

As a matter of fact Bobbie Chermbacon and the Marchioness travelled up to Town by the same train. He had grasped the fact that his presence was not in request at either of the house-parties, and she was hurriedly summoned to London, where her husband had entered on the illness which, in a few days, made her a widow and a dowager. Bobbie's enthusiasm for chestnut hair and dreamy Madonna eyes did not lead him to repeat his visit to the Duff-Chubleigh household. He spent the winter in Egypt, and some ten months later he married the widowed Marchioness.

The Bystander, 9th July, 1913

THE HOLY WAR

Revil Yealmton sat in the swaying dining-car of a Nord Express train that raced westward through the Prussian plain in the dusk of an early summer day. After nearly two years of profitable business pilgrimage in the border regions of Asiatic Russia he was returning to wife and home in the English West Country. It was a house that, as a matter of fact, he had never inhabited, and yet he was looking forward to reaching it as eagerly as though it had been the hallowed dwelling place of his childhood. Old memories endeared the place to his recollection, even though they were the memories of one who had dreamed rather than of one who had experienced. In his early days, when he had lived with his parents in a prim and rather dreary cottage in a sleepy West Country village, the old gabled house at the foot of the hill had been occupied by a bachelor uncle, who had not encouraged his relatives to intrude too freely on his seclusion. From the evergreen fastness of a conveniently placed holly hedge the boy had been able to look, unobserved, on the domain with which he seldom enjoyed closer acquaintance, and in his eyes it had been a wonderful and desirable abode for mortal man. Every detail stood up in his mind now with undimmed distinctness as he sat finishing his dinner in the jolting train. There was the broad pond at the entrance, whereupon a company of drakes and ducks, mottled and ringstraked and burnished, went to and fro like a flotilla of painted merchantmen on an inland sea; there were high white gates that led into a yew-begirt garden on one side and a wide straw-yard on the other, a yard in which radiant-plumaged gamecocks led their attendant trains of hen folk in endless busy forays, and sleek, damson-hued pigs grubbed and munched and dozed the day long. And on the hillside beyond the yard there was an orchard of unspeakable delight, where the goldfinches nested in the spring, and the apples and greengages and cherries made one's eyes ache with longing in fruit time. There were a hundred other heart-enslaving things that he remembered from his boyhood's days, and the wonder was that the clamour of them had stood the critical test of maturing years. After his parents had passed into a pious memory he had revisited the neighbourhood with the assurance of a successful mercantile career to his credit, and had found the old uncle more humane and friendly than of yore, and the old gabled house and all that stood with it as bewitching as ever. And then, a few months later, as he had been setting out on his important eastward journey, the uncle had died and left his nephew all that earthly paradise to have and to hold. Yealmton had sent his wife to take possession, and deferred the joy of entering into his desired land until he should have seen his Russian enterprise to a successful conclusion. And now he was returning, with a riot of expectant longing in his brain, to his home — and to Thirza. But a thought kept intruding itself with unwelcome cynicism: was his wife really included in the anticipations that piled themselves so pleasantly before him?

Thirza Yealmton was what is known as a managing woman. Of such there are many that are only to be spoken of with honour and incense-burning, but Thirza was of the regrettable kind that can never realise that nature, and particularly human nature, is sometimes devised and constructed to be unmanageable, for its own happiness and its own good. Yealmton thought, with a suppressed psalm of thanksgiving at the back of his mind, of the comfortable discomfort of his last two years of travel, and of how Thirza's presence on the scene would assuredly have entailed a distressing accompaniment of arranging and supervising and general dislocation of the accepted way of things. He knew that he was impatiently counting the slow hours that separated him from the old homestead at the foot of the hill, but he could not reassure himself that any of the impatience was honestly due to a desire to be once more in his wife's company and within the sphere of her organising genius.

Later, when Thirza met him with the pony-cart at the small country station, Yealmton knew that his cynical self-accusation had been well founded. The anticipation still ran high in his brain and heart, none of it had found realisation in the meeting with his wife. It was unfortunate, he admitted to himself, but he was too engrossed with other crowding sensations to give the matter more than a perfunctory vote of censure. He hardly heeded Thirza's unstemmed torrent of talk that kept pace with the rattle of pony's hoofs, until a sentence detached itself with unpleasant distinctness.

"You will find a lot of improvements since you last saw the place."

"Improvements?"

He jerked out the question wonderingly. It had never crossed his mind that any improvement could be desirable in the wonderland that he remembered.

"For one thing," said Thirza, as the cart swung round a corner and brought them into view of the gates, "I've had that old pond at the entrance drained away; it made things damp and looked untidy."

Yealmton said nothing, and Thirza did not see the look that came into his eyes. He remained silent, too, when his wife introduced him to a monotonous colony of white Leghorns, in wired runs, that she had substituted for the lively poultry yard of strutting, gorgon-hued game fowl that had been his uncle's special pride.

"The miller bought most of the old stock," she informed him: "a quarrelsome straying lot those game fowl were. I was glad to get rid of them. These ones are record layers, and I make quite a lot by their eggs. This is where the orchard was."

She showed him a trim array of young fruit trees, planted in serried rows, in a carefully wooded enclosure.

"When they are fully grown they will yield three times the profit that the old orchard did," she observed.

"We are not poor," said Yealmton.

Thirza was chilled and offended; how little her husband appreciated the trouble she had been to in the matter.

"Money is always worth having," she said sharply.

"Goldfinches used to build in the old orchard," said Yealmton, almost to himself.

"Birds are a mistake about a garden, I think," said Thirza: "we could have goldfinches in an aviary if you liked."

"I would not like," said Yealmton, shortly.

A yellow figure came down a garden path and made straight for the newcomer.

"Hullo, Peterkin," cried Yealmton, gladly, and a golden-furred cat sprang purring into his arms.

"How funny!" said Thirza. "That cat hasn't been seen anywhere about the place since the first week I was here; I didn't know it was still in existence. Don't let it come into the house," she added; "I don't encourage cats about a house."

For answer Yealmton carried Peterkin into the morning-room and placed him on a broad shelf built into the ingle-nook.

"That was his throne in my uncle's time," he said: "It is his throne now."

Thirza promptly decided on a four days' headache, which was her invariable recipe whenever anyone thwarted or annoyed her. She had been known to postpone it in times of stress, such as Christmas week or a spring cleaning, but she would never forgo it altogether. For the moment she said nothing.

After dinner that evening Yealmton stood at an open window, with Peterkin purring rapturously at his side, and listened for some remembered sound that should have come to him through the dusk.

"Why aren't the wood owls hooting?" he asked. "They always used to call from the copse about this time. All the way across Europe I've been longing to hear those owls singing Vespers."

"Do you like their noise?" asked Thirza. "I couldn't stand it. I got the local gamekeeper to shoot them. It was such a dismal noise, I think."

"Is there any other vile thing that you have done in this dear old place?" asked Yealmton. He spoke to himself, but he asked the question aloud. Then he added: "Something dreadful must surely happen to you!"

Thirza gasped and stared at him for half a minute.

"You are over-tired with your journey," she said at last, and went upstairs to inaugurate a headache, which, she felt, could scarcely last less than a week.

Judicious digging operations restored the pond to something like its old splendour, and a great company of ducks, mottled and ringstraked and speckled, went to and fro on its waters as though they had been doing it all their lives. A couple of young gamecocks, supplied by the sympathetic miller, made short work of the alien white cockerels that had reigned in their stead, and the local gamekeeper was warned of the dismal things that would befall him if any further owl slaughter was brought home to his account. Even the fruit paddock was induced to lose some of its nursery-garden air and to stray back toward the glory of a West Country orchard. The birds of heaven received no further discouragement, except such as was meted out to them by Peterkin in his capacity of warden of the currant bushes. And while these things were being done Yealmton and his wife waged a politely reticent warfare; it was a struggle which Thirza knew she must ultimately win, because she was fighting for existence — arranging and interfering and supervising were a necessary condition of her well-being. What she did not know, or did not understand, was that

Yealmton was fighting a Holy War, and therefore could not be defeated.

As summer and autumn passed away into winter Thirza turned her managing energies in a greater degree upon the rural life of the village, where she encountered less formidable obstacles than Yealmton's overruling opposition presented in the narrower sphere. She was not popular with the cottagers, but she had thoroughly mastered the art of being penetrating.

"I am going down to the mill-ponds," she announced one afternoon, when a hard frost had held the land for a couple of days; "the children will be coming out of school about now. They've been warned not to go on the ice, and I mean to see that they don't."

"It can't possibly bear yet," said Yealmton.

"It bears at the shallow end," said Thirza.

"Then why not let them go on the shallow end?" asked Yealmton.

"They've been told not to," said Thirza; "I don't wish to argue the matter. I mean to see that none of them go on."

As a matter of fact the children were engrossed with a slide at the other end of the village, and Thirza had the lonely mill meadows to herself. From the orchard gate

Yealmton could see her walking rapidly along the reed-fringed borders of the wide ponds, as though determined to see no adventurous urchin was enjoying a furtive slide in some hidden nook among the bushes. As he watched the dark, solitary figure moving through the desolate wintry waste his involuntary prophecy shot across his mind: "Something dreadful must surely happen to you." And at that moment her saw something white rush out of the bushes and come flapping towards her, he saw Thirza start back, and fall on the slippery edge of the pond, and across the meadows a scream came on the frozen air. It was a long while before he could reach the spot, running at his highest speed, and when he arrived the woman was lying half under the scum of churned-up ice and slush at the pond's edge, and something white and ghostly was stealing away through the dusk. Yealmton knew it for a wild swan, wounded by some gunner on the coast, and harbouring among the reeds till it should die; savage and weak with hunger and death-fear, but with strength enough left to do — what it had done.

The Morning Post, 6th May, 1913

THE ALMANAC — a Clovis story

"Has it ever struck you," said Vera Durmot to Clovis, "that one might make a comfortable income by compiling a local almanack, on prophetic lines, like those that the general public buy by the half million?"

"An income, perhaps," said Clovis, "but not a comfortable one. The prophet has proverbially a thin sort of time in his own country, and you would be too closely mixed up with the people you were prophesying about to be able to get much comfort out of the job. If the man who foretells tragic happenings for the Crowned Heads of Europe had to meet them at luncheon parties and tea-fights every other day of the week he would not find his business a comfortable one, especially towards the last days of the year, when the tragedies were getting overdue."

"I should sell it just before the New Year," said Vera, ignoring the suggestion of possible embarrassment, "at eighteenpence a copy, and get a friend to type it for me, so that every copy I sold would be clear profit. Everyone would buy it out of curiosity, just to see how many of the predictions would be falsified."

"Wouldn't it be rather a trying time for you later on," asked Clovis, "when the predictions began to 'lack confirmation'?"

"The thing would be," said Vera, "to arrange your forecast so that it couldn't go very far wrong. I should begin with the prediction that the vicar would preach a moving New Year sermon from a text in Colossians; he has always done so since I can remember, and at his time of life men dislike change. Then one could safely foretell for the month of January that 'more than one well-known family in this neighbourhood will be faced with a serious financial outlook which, however, will not develop into actual crisis.' Every other head of a family down here discovers about that time of year that his household is living far beyond its income, and that severe retrenchment will be necessary. For April or May or thereabouts I should hint that one of the Dibcuster girls would make the happiest choice of her life. There are eight of them, and it's really time that one of the family married or went on the stage or took to writing worldly novels."

"They have never done anything of the kind within human memory," objected Clovis.

"One must take some risks," said Vera. "I should be on safer ground," she added, "in predicting serious servant troubles from February to November. 'Some of the best mistresses and house managers in this locality will be faced with vexatious servant difficulties, which will be temporarily tided over.' "

"Another safe forecast," suggested Clovis, "could be fitted into the dates when there are medal competitions at the golf club. 'One or two of the most brilliant local players will encounter extraordinary and persistent bad luck, which will rob them of the deserved guerdon of good play.' At least a dozen men will think your prophecies positively inspired."

Vera made a note of the suggestion.

"I'll let you have an advance copy at half price," she said; "on the other hand, I expect you to see that your mother buys one at market rates."

"She shall buy two," said Clovis; "she can give one to Lady Adela, who never buys anything that she can borrow."

The almanack had a big sale, and most of its predictions came sufficiently near fulfilment to sustain the compiler's claim to prophetic powers of an eighteenpenny standard. One of the Dibcuster girls made up her mind to be a hospital nurse and another of them gave up piano playing, both of which might be considered happy decisions, while the forecast of servant troubles and unmerited bad luck on the golf links received ample confirmation in the annals of the home and the club.

"I don't see how she was to know that I was going to change my cook twice in seven months," said Mrs. Duff, who easily recognised an allusion to herself as one of the best mistresses of the neighbourhood.

"And it's come quite true about phenomenal vegetable products being recorded from a local garden," said Mrs. Openshaw; "it said 'a garden which has long been the admiration of the neighbourhood for its magnificent flowers will this year produce some marvels in the way of vegetables.' Our garden is the admiration of everybody, and yesterday Henry brought in some carrots, well, you wouldn't see anything to equal them at a show."

"Oh, but I think that refers to our garden," said Mrs. Duff, "it has always been admired for its flowers, and now we've got some Glory of the South parsnips that beat anything I've ever seen. We've taken their measurements, and I got Phyllis to photograph them. I shall certainly buy the almanack if it comes out another year."

"I've ordered it already," said Mrs. Openshaw; "after what it foretold about my garden I thought I ought to."

While the general verdict was in favour of the almanack as an inspired production, or, at any rate, a very fair compilation of successful prediction, there were critics who pointed out that most of the events foretold were of the nature of things that happened in one form or another in any given year.

"I couldn't risk being very definite about any particular event," said Vera to Clovis towards the end of the twelve-month; "as it is I have rather tied myself up over Jocelyn Vanner. I hinted that the hunting field was not a safe place for her during November and December. It is never a safe place for her at any time, she is always coming off a jump or getting bolted with or something of that sort. And now she has taken alarm at my prediction, and only comes to the meets on foot. Nothing very serious can happen to her under those circumstances."

"It must be ruining her hunting season," said Clovis.

"It's ruining the reputation of my almanack," said Vera; "it's the one thing that has definitely miscarried. I felt so sure she would have a spill of some sort that could be magnified into a serious accident."

"I'm afraid I can't offer to ride over her, or incite hounds to tear her to pieces in mistake for a fox," said Clovis; "I should earn your undying devotion, but there would be a wearisome fuss about it, and I should have to hunt with another pack in future, and that would be dreadfully inconvenient."

"As your mother says, you are a mass of selfishness," commented Vera.

An opportunity for being unselfish occurred to Clovis a day or two later, when he found himself at close quarters with Jocelyn near Bludberry Gate, where hounds were drawing a long woody hollow in search of an elusive fox.

"Scent is poor, and there's an interminable amount of cover," grumbled Clovis from his saddle; "we shall be here for hours before we get a fox away."

"All the more time for you to talk to me," said Jocelyn archly.

"The question is," said Clovis darkly, "whether I ought to be seen talking to you. I may be involving you."

"Heavens! Involving me in what?" gasped Jocelyn.

"Do you know anything about Bukowina?" Clovis asked with seeming inconsequence.

"Bukowina? It's somewhere in Asia Minor, isn't it — or Central Asia — or is it part of the Balkans?" hazarded Jocelyn; "I really forget for the moment. Where exactly is it?"

"On the brink of a revolution," said Clovis impressively; "that's what I want to warn you about. When I was staying with my aunt in Bucharest" (Clovis invented aunts as lavishly as other people invent golfing experiences) "I got mixed up in the affair without knowing what I was in for. There was a Princess–"

"Ah," said Jocelyn knowingly, "there always is a beautiful and alluring Princess in these affairs."

"As plain and boring a woman as one could find in Eastern Europe," said Clovis; "one of the sort that call just before lunch and stay till it's time to dress for dinner. Well, it seems that some Rumanian Jew is willing to finance the revolution if he can be assured of getting certain mineral concessions. The Jew is cruising in a yacht somewhere off the English coast, and the Princess had made up her mind that I was the safest person to convey the concession papers to him. My aunt whispered, 'For Heaven's sake agree to what she says or she'll stay on to dinner.' At that moment any sacrifice seemed better than that, and so here I am, with my breast pocket bulging with compromising documents, and my life not worth a minute's purchase."

"But," said Jocelyn, "you are safe here in England, aren't you?"

"Do you see that man over there, on the roan?" asked Clovis, pointing to a man with a heavy black moustache, who was probably an auctioneer from a neighbouring town, and at any rate was a stranger to the hunt. "That man was outside my aunt's house when I escorted the Princess to her carriage. He was on the platform of the railway station when I left Bucharest. He was on the landing-stage when I arrived in England. I can go nowhere without finding him at my elbow. I was not surprised to see him at the meet this morning."

"But what can he do to you?" asked Jocelyn tremulously; "he can't kill you."

"Not before witnesses, if he can avoid it. The moment hounds find and the field scatters will be his opportunity. He means to have those papers to-day."

"But how can he be sure you've got them on you?"

"He can't; I might have slipped them over to you while we were talking. That is why he is trying to make up his mind which of us to go for at the critical moment."

"Us?" screamed Jocelyn; "do you mean to say–?"

"I warned you that it was dangerous to be seen talking to me."

"But this awful! What am I to do?"

"Slip away into the undergrowth the moment that hounds get moving, and run like a rabbit. It is your only chance, and remember, if you escape, no talking. Many lives will be involved if you breathe a word of what I've told you. My aunt at Bucharest–"

At that moment there was a whimper from hounds down in the hollow, and a general ripple of movement passed through the scattered groups of waiting horsemen. A louder and more assured burst of noise came up from the valley.

"They've found!" cried Clovis and turned eagerly to join in the stampede. A crashing, scrunching noise as of a body rapidly and resolutely forcing its way through birch thicket and dead bracken was all that remained to him of his late companion.

Jocelyn's most intimate friends never knew the exact nature of the deadly peril she had incurred in the hunting field that day, but enough was made known to ensure the almanack a brisk sale at its new price of three shillings.

The Morning Post, 17th June, 1913

The East Wing

IT was early February and the hour was somewhere about two in the morning. Most of the house-party had retired to bed. Lucien Wattleskeat had merely retired to his bedroom where he sat over the still vigorous old-age of a fire, balancing the entries in his bridge-book. They worked out at seventy-eight shillings on the right side, as the result of two evenings' play, which was not so bad, considering that the stakes had been regrettably low.

Lucien was a young man who regarded himself with an undemonstrative esteem, which the undiscerning were apt to mistake for indifference. Several women of his acquaintance were on the look-out for nice girls for him to marry, a vigil in which he took no share.

The atmosphere of the room was subtly tinged with an essence of tuberose, and more strongly impregnated with the odour of wood-fire smoke. Lucien noticed this latter circumstance as he finished his bridge-audit, and also noticed that the fire in the grate was not a wood one, neither was it smoking.

A stronger smell of smoke blew into the room a moment later as the door opened, and Major Boventry, pyjama-clad and solemnly excited, stood in the doorway.

"The house is on fire!" he exclaimed.

"Oh," said Lucien, "is that it? I thought perhaps you had come to talk to me. If you would shut the door the smoke wouldn't pour in so."

"We ought to do something," said the Major with conviction.

"I hardly know the family," said Lucien, "but I suppose one will be expected to be present, even though the fire does not appear to be in this wing of the house."

"It may spread to here," said the Major.

"Well, let's go and look at it," assented Lucien, "though it's against my principles to meet trouble half-way."

"Grasp your nettle, that's what I say," observed Boventry.

"In this case, Major, it's not our nettle," retorted Lucien, carefully shutting the bedroom door behind him.

In the passage they encountered Canon Clore, arrayed in a dressing-gown of Albanian embroidery, which might have escaped remark in a Te Deum service in the Cathedral of the Assumption at Moscow, but which looked out of place in the corridor of an English country house. But then, as Lucien observed to himself, at a fire one can wear anything.

"The house is on fire," said the Canon, with the air of one who lends dignity to a fact by according it gracious recognition.

"It's in the east wing, I think," said the Major.

"I suppose it is another case of suffragette militancy," said the Canon. "I am in favour of women having the vote myself, even if, as some theologians assert, they have no souls. That, indeed, would furnish an additional argument for including them in the electorate, so that all sections of the community, the soulless and the souled, might be represented, and, being in favour of the female vote, I am naturally in favour of militant means to achieve it. Belonging as I do to a Church Militant, I should be inconsistent if I professed to stand aghast at militant methods in vote-winning warfare. But, at the same time, I cannot resist pointing out that the women who are using violent means to wring the vote-right from a reluctant legislature are destroying the value of the very thing for which they are struggling. A vote is of no conceivable consequence to anybody unless it carries with it the implicit understanding that majority-rule is the settled order of the day, and the militants are actively engaged in demonstrating that any minority armed with a box of matches and a total disregard of consequences can force its opinions and its wishes on an indifferent or hostile community. It is not merely manor-houses that they are destroying, but the whole fabric of government by ballot-box."

"Oughtn't we to be doing something about the fire?" said Major Boventry.

"I was going to suggest something of the sort myself," said the Canon stiffly.

"Tomorrow may be too late, as the advertisements in the newspapers say," observed Lucien.

In the hall they met their hostess, Mrs Gramplain.

"I'm so glad you have come," she said; "servants are so little help in an emergency of this kind. My husband has gone off in the car to summon the fire-brigade."

"Haven't you telephoned to them?" asked the Major.

"The telephone unfortunately is in the east wing," said the hostess; "so is the telephone-book. Both are being devoured by the flames at this moment. It makes one feel dreadfully isolated. Now if the fire had only broken out in the west wing instead, we could have used the telephone and had the fire-engines here by now."

"On the other hand," objected Lucien, "Canon Clore and Major Boventry and myself would probably have met with the fate that has overtaken the telephone-book. I think I prefer the present arrangement."

"The butler and most of the other servants are in the dining-room, trying to save the Raeburns and the alleged

Van Dyke," continued Mrs Gramplain, "and in that little room on the first landing, cut off from us by the cruel flames, is my poor darling Eva ? Eva of the golden hair. Will none of you save her?"

"Who is Eva of the golden hair?" asked Lucien.

"My daughter," said Mrs Gramplain.

"I didn't know you had a daughter," said Lucien, "and really I don't think I can risk my life to save some one I've never met or even heard about. You see, my life is not only wonderful and beautiful to myself, but if my life goes, nothing else really matters ? to me. I don't suppose you can realise that, to me, the whole world as it exists to-day, the Ulster problem, the Albanian tangle, the Kikuyu controversy, the wide field of social reform and Antarctic exploration, the realms of finance, and research and international armaments, all this varied and crowded and complex world, all comes to a complete and absolute end the moment my life is finished. Eva might be snatched from the flames and live to be the grandmother of brilliant and charming men and women; but, as far as I should be concerned, she and they would no more exist than a vanished puff of cigarette smoke or a dissolved soda-water bubble. And if, in losing my life, I am to lose her life and theirs, as far as I personally am concerned with them, why on earth should I, personally, risk my life to save hers and theirs?"

"Major Boventry," exclaimed Mrs Gramplain, "you are not clever, but you are a man with honest human feelings. I have only known you for a few hours, but I am sure you are the man I take you for. You will not let my Eva perish."

"Lady," said the Major stumblingly, "I would gladly give my life to rescue your Eva, or anybody's Eva for the matter of that, but my life is not mine to give. I am engaged to the sweetest little woman in the world. I am everything to her. What would my poor little Mildred say if they brought her news that I had cast away my life in an endeavour, perhaps fruitless, to save some unknown girl in a burning country house?"

"You are like all the rest of them," said Mrs Gramplain bitterly; "I thought that you, at least, were stupid. It shows how rash it is to judge a man by his bridge-play. It has been like this all my life," she continued in dull, level tones; "I was married, when little more than a child, to my husband, and there has never been any real bond of affection between us. We have been polite and considerate to one another, nothing more. I sometimes think that if we had had a child things might have been different."

"But ? your daughter Eva?" queried the Canon, and the two other men echoed his question.

"I have never had a daughter," said the woman quietly, yet, amid the roar and crackle of the flames, her voice carried, so that not a syllable was lost. "Eva is the outcome of my imagination. I so much wanted a little girl, and at last I came to believe that she really existed. She grew up, year by year, in my mind, and when she was eighteen I painted her portrait, a beautiful young girl with masses of golden hair. Since that moment the portrait has been Eva. I have altered it a little with the changing years ? she is twenty-one now ? and I have repainted her dress with every incoming fashion. On her last birthday I painted her a pair of beautiful diamond earrings. Every day I have sat with her for an hour or so, telling her my thoughts, or reading to her. And now she is there, alone with the flames and the smoke, unable to stir, waiting for the deliverance that does not come."

"It is beautiful," said Lucien; "it is the most beautiful thing I ever heard."

"Where are you going?" asked his hostess, as the young man moved towards the blazing staircase of the east wing.

"I am going to try and save her," he answered; "as she has never existed, my death cannot compromise her future existence. I shall go into nothingness, and she, as far as I am concerned, will go into nothingness too; but then she has never been anything else."

"But your life, your beautiful life?"

"Death in this case is more beautiful."

The Major started forward.

"I am going too," he said simply.

"To save Eva?" cried the woman.

"Yes," he said; "my little Mildred will not grudge me to a woman who has never existed."

"How well he reads our sex," murmured Mrs Gramplain, "and yet how badly he plays bridge!"

The two men went side by side up the blazing staircase, the slender young figure in the well-fitting dinner-jacket and the thick-set military man in striped pyjamas of an obvious Swan & Edgar pattern. Down in the hall below them stood the woman in her pale wrapper, and the Canon in his wonderful-hued Albanian-work dressing-gown, looking like the arch-priests of some strange religion presiding at a human sacrifice.

As the rescue-party disappeared into the roaring cavern of smoke and flames, the butler came into the hall, bearing with him one of the Raeburns.

"I think I hear the clanging of the fire-engines, ma'am," he announced.

Mrs Gramplain continued staring at the spot where the two men had disappeared.

"How stupid of me!" she said presently to the Canon. "I've just remembered I sent Eva to Exeter to be cleaned. Those two men have lost their lives for nothing."

"They have certainly lost their lives," said the Canon.

"The irony of it all," said Mrs Gramplain, "the tragic irony of it all!"

"The real irony of the affair lies in the fact that it will be instrumental in working a social revolution of the utmost magnitude," said the Canon. "When it becomes known, through the length and breadth of the land, that an army officer and a young ornament of the social world have lost their lives in a country-house fire, started by suffragette incendiarism, the conscience of the country will be aroused, and people will cry out that the price is too heavy to pay. The militants will be in worse odour than ever, but, like the Importunate Widow, they will get their way. Over the charred bodies of Major Boventry and Lucien Wattleskeat the banners of progress and enfranchisement will be carried forward to victory, and the mothers of the nation will henceforth take their part in electing the Mother of Parliaments. England will range herself with Finland and other enlightened countries which have already admitted women to the labours, honours, and responsibilities of the polling-booth. In the early hours of this February morning a candle has been lighted ? "

"The fire was caused by an over-heated flue, and not by suffragettes, sir," interposed the butler.

At that moment a scurry of hoofs and a clanging of bells, together with the hoot of a motor-horn, were heard above the roaring of the flames.

"The fire-brigade!" exclaimed the Canon.

"The fire-brigade and my husband," said Mrs Gramplain, in her dull level voice; "it will all begin over again now, the old life, the old unsatisfying weariness, the old monotony; nothing will be changed."

"Except the east wing," said the Canon gently.